Hiding Hoover

by **Elise Broach**

pictures by **Laura Huliska-Beith**

Dial Books for Young Readers
New York

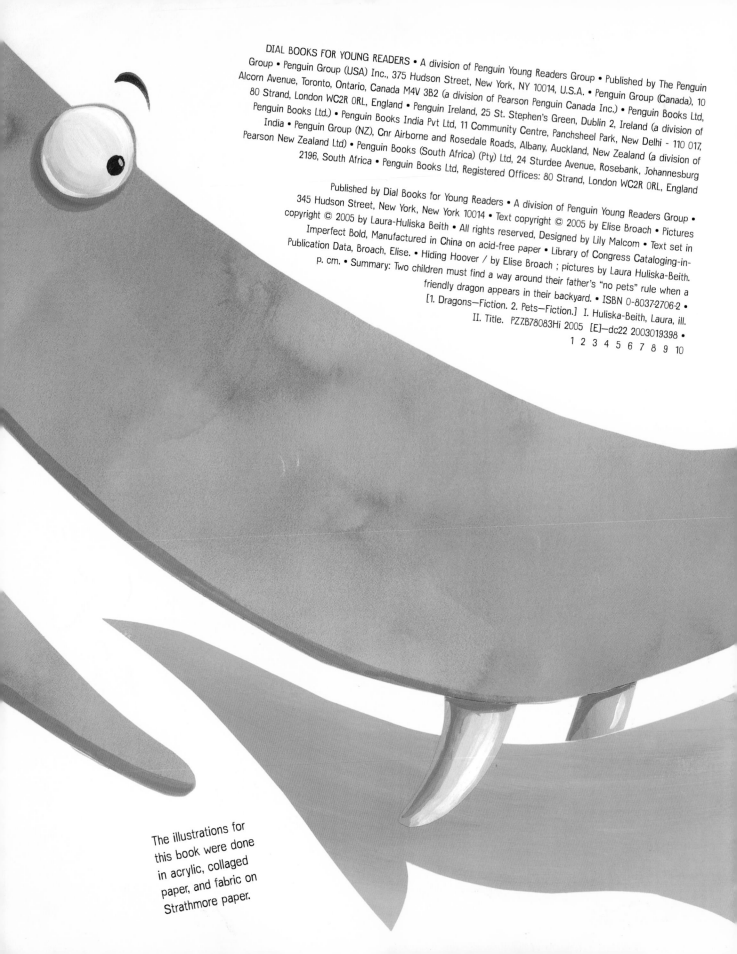

DIAL BOOKS FOR YOUNG READERS • A division of Penguin Young Readers Group • Published by The Penguin Group • Penguin Group (USA) Inc., 375 Hudson Street, New York, NY 10014, U.S.A. • Penguin Group (Canada), 10 Alcorn Avenue, Toronto, Ontario, Canada M4V 3B2 (a division of Pearson Penguin Canada Inc.) • Penguin Books Ltd, 80 Strand, London WC2R 0RL, England • Penguin Ireland, 25 St. Stephen's Green, Dublin 2, Ireland (a division of Penguin Books Ltd.) • Penguin Books India Pvt Ltd, 11 Community Centre, Panchsheel Park, New Delhi - 110 017, India • Penguin Group (NZ), Cnr Airborne and Rosedale Roads, Albany, Auckland, New Zealand (a division of Pearson New Zealand Ltd) • Penguin Books (South Africa) (Pty) Ltd, 24 Sturdee Avenue, Rosebank, Johannesburg 2196, South Africa • Penguin Books Ltd, Registered Offices: 80 Strand, London WC2R 0RL, England

Published by Dial Books for Young Readers • A division of Penguin Young Readers Group • 345 Hudson Street, New York, New York 10014 • Text copyright © 2005 by Elise Broach • Pictures copyright © 2005 by Laura-Huliska Beith • All rights reserved, Designed by Lily Malcom • Text set in Imperfect Bold, Manufactured in China on acid-free paper • Library of Congress Cataloging-in-Publication Data, Broach, Elise. • Hiding Hoover / by Elise Broach ; pictures by Laura Huliska-Beith. p. cm. • Summary: Two children must find a way around their father's "no pets" rule when a friendly dragon appears in their backyard. • ISBN 0-8037-2706-2 • [1. Dragons—Fiction. 2. Pets—Fiction.] I. Huliska-Beith, Laura, ill. II. Title. PZ7.B78083Hi 2005 [E]—dc22 2003019398 • 1 2 3 4 5 6 7 8 9 10

The illustrations for this book were done in acrylic, collaged paper, and fabric on Strathmore paper.

For Zoe
—E.B.

For my animal-lovin' pals and their
people-lovin' animals.
And for my own four-legged motley crew.
(Including my two-legged husband.)
—L.H-B.

Daddy always said, "No pets."
No puppies or parakeets, cats or
canaries, gerbils or turtles or mice.

No pets. **NO PETS.**

But then we found Hoover.

On a dark, rainy day, there he was, eating dandelions in our backyard. He had horns on his head, and spikes on his back, and a tail that swept through the grass when he walked . . .

swish, swish, swish.

We stared at him, and he stared at us. He looked hungry, and lost, and a little bit shy. And then, with a *whoosh,* he spread his big wings, and we thought: Oh, no! Don't fly away!

So we talked softly to him, and tossed crackers to
him, and called him in out of the rain. And he came
when we called, through the grass and the rain . . .

Swish, swish, *swish.*

That's when we knew. We had to have Hoover.
And we had to hide Hoover.

Daddy would be home soon!

We put him in bed and tucked him under
the blankets. We pulled the sheets and
smoothed the bedspread, but . . .

Hoover was too spiky to hide in a bed.

So we stuffed him into the closet.
We pushed the hangers around, and
we squeezed and we squished, but . . .

Hoover was too long to hide in a closet.

So we dressed him up like one of our friends.

Hoover liked how he looked in a sweater and hat, but . . .

he was too flappy to hide in our clothes.

Daddy would be home soon. We had to hide Hoover!
But where?

We thought, and we thought, and we thought—

mm-hmm . . . **oh-ho** . . .

When Daddy walked in that night, there was a new
coat stand in our hallway. He hung up his jacket on one
of the hooks. Then he tossed his hat on it . . . *cr-runch!*

Daddy didn't notice a thing.

Then Daddy needed something from the top shelf of the cupboard. We showed him how to climb our new stepladder, and how to slide back down too . . .

BUMP-slip, BUMP-slip, BUMP!

When we sat down to dinner, a fancy new lamp with a flickery flame hung over our heads. It got so hot, we thought we were going to melt . . . *huffaluff, huffaluff, huff!*

Daddy didn't notice a thing.

After dinner we took out our handy new vacuum cleaner. With a *whisk, whisssk, WHISSSKKK,* we cleaned up the floor, till every last crumb was gone.

Then we all took a walk in the rain. What would we have done without our big flappy umbrella? It flipped and flapped so much, we were afraid it might fly away . . .

flippity, flappity, flap!

Daddy didn't notice a thing.

At bedtime, we sat with Daddy in our comfy new reading chair. When the story got exciting, it *rr*-rolled and *rr*-rumbled. We fell off twice! ***Thump! Thump!***

Later that night, when we crawled into bed, we had a frilly new canopy stretching over us. It made soft sounds in the warm, green dark . . .

hah-S w i s h, hah-s w i s h, hah-s w i s h.

So we went to sleep happy, because we had Hoover. And Daddy *never* noticed a thing!